MICHAEL BROAD

MINNEAPOLIS

American edition published in 2011 by Darby Creek,
a division of Lerner Publishing Group, Inc.

Copyright © 2007 by Michael Broad

First published in 2007 by Andersen Press Limited,
20 Vauxhall Bridge Road, London SW1V 2SA
www.andersenpress.co.uk   www.michaelbroad.co.uk

Darby Creek
A division of Lerner Publishing Group, Inc.
241 First Avenue North
Minneapolis, MN 55401 U.S.A.

Website address: www.lernerbooks.com

Library of Congress Cataloging-in-Publication Data

Broad, Michael.
    Zombie cows! / written and illustrated by Michael Broad. — 1st American ed.
        v. cm. — (Agent Amelia, #2)
    Summary: Amelia, a young secret agent, investigates some robotic animals, an enchanting music teacher, and a pair of remarkably beautiful twin bakers with a dastardly plot, all while avoiding her nemesis, Trudy Hart.
    Contents: The case of the zombie cows — The case of the perilous pipe — The case of the creepy cakes.
    ISBN: 978–0–7613–8057–3 (lib. bdg. : alk. paper)
    [1. Spies—Fiction. 2. Robots—Fiction. 3. Music teachers—Fiction.
4. Teachers—Fiction. 5. Bakers and bakeries—Fiction.] I. Title.
PZ7.B780834Zom 2011
[E]—dc22   2011001089

Manufactured in the United States of America
1 – BP – 7/15/11

For Cheryl

The Case of the
Zombie Cows   11

The Case of the
Perilous Pipe   55

The Case of the
Creepy Cakes   97

I'M AMELIA KIDD and I'm a secret agent.

Well, I'm not actually a secret agent. I don't work for the government or anything. But I've saved the world loads of times from evil geniuses and criminal masterminds. There are loads of them around if you know what to look for.

I'm really good at disguises. I make my own gadgets (which sometimes work), and I'm used to improvising in sticky situations—which you have to do all the time when you're a secret agent.

These are my Secret Agent Case Files.

The Case of the Zombie Cows

During the holidays, when Mom's not
working, we go out for the day.
Usually we try to go somewhere
different. Most times
we end up
somewhere really
cool, but other
times we end up
somewhere not
so cool.

This time Mom decided on the local petting zoo. Which is cool if you're really young—but not so cool if you're a secret agent who has definitely grown out of fluffy bunny rabbits.

I admit I was sulking when we arrived. I was huffing and puffing as we made our way down the gravel path toward the farmyard. Unfortunately, Mom saw this as an opportunity for a bit of interrogation.

"Amelia, why, oh why, do you insist on dragging that big heavy bag everywhere we go?" she said, jabbing a finger at my backpack. "Just what do you think you'll need?"

"Stuff," I said, eyeing her carefully over the top of my sunglasses. Mom eyed me back.

Sometimes saying "stuff" will cover it and Mom won't bother to check what's inside my backpack. But my mom is pretty smart, and every so often, curiosity gets the better of her.

"What kind of stuff exactly?" she asked.

"Drawing stuff," I said innocently.

"So I can draw the fluffy bunny rabbits."

Mom immediately raised a suspicious eyebrow. I'd obviously gone too far with the fluffy bunny rabbits. Now I was going to have to prove it or bring unwanted attention to my secret-agent activities.

With the biggest sigh I could manage, I heaved off my backpack. I unzipped the flap, pulled out a drawing book and a handful of pencils, and waved them in the air. Of course the rest of my bag was stuffed with secret-agent stuff,

but in the last week I'd seen Mom grow more curious about my backpack and had packed the book and pencils just in case.

You have to think ahead when you're a secret agent.

"I didn't need to see them," Mom shrugged innocently. "I was just making conversation."

As I suspected, the petting zoo wasn't very interesting.

The animals were cute, but they were all small and fluffy. I couldn't really see them anyway because there were lots of other kids crowding around—kids that were at least half my age!

To make matters worse, Mom bumped into an old friend and was chatting for ages. I slunk away to look for some bigger, more grown-up animals like horses or elephants. OK, I didn't really expect to find an elephant, but it was a farm, so there could be a horse.

I was in luck—
as soon as I
turned the
corner,

climbed a couple of fences, and
negotiated my way through some
bushes, I eventually found the stables.

But my luck quickly ran
out as very loud voice
stopped me in my tracks.

"AMELIA KIDD!
WHAT ON EARTH
ARE *YOU* DOING
HERE?"

At first I thought Mom had seen me sneaking off, followed me, and planned to march me back to the fluffy bunny rabbits. But then I realized the voice was much too high-pitched and whiny—which could mean only one other person.

I turned around slowly to see Trudy Hart. She was storming across the courtyard in riding coat, boots, and hat, and waving her crop at me.

Trudy is in my class at school, and we
don't get along. In fact, we're sworn
enemies.

"Well?" she demanded, eyeing
me up and down with her nose high
in the air.

Because she took me by
surprise, I was about to explain that I
was bored with the petting zoo and

was looking for something more interesting to pet. But then I thought of a better response.

"It's none of your business!" I yelled.

"My daddy owns these stables, so I think it is my business!" she snapped.

"Oh," I said, lowering my voice and forcing my mouth into a fake smile. "I wasn't doing any harm. I just wanted to see the horses."

"They're not *rocking* horses. They're intelligent animals, and I forbid you from going anywhere near them!"

Trudy sneered and thrust her riding crop in the direction of a nearby field.

"I will allow you to see the cows, though. They're awfully stupid, so you'll probably find you have a lot in common!"

I was about to raise my voice again when a short, thin man appeared from one of the stables. My secret-agent senses immediately kicked in when I noticed the man was carrying a shiny black briefcase!

Evil geniuses and criminal masterminds often carry briefcases to hold their fiendish plans for world domination. That doesn't mean *everyone* who has a  briefcase is planning to take over the world, but this man was obviously just a stable hand, which made it *very* suspicious.

"Lightning is ready for you, Miss Trudy," he said.

The man caught me peering at
him over my sunglasses. He narrowed
his eyes, making him look like an
angry gnome. "Is everything OK, Miss
Trudy?" he added cautiously.

"Yes, thank you, Albert," said
Trudy, without looking around. "One
of those dreadful petting-zoo people
got lost again. I said she could go and
gawk at the cows."

"But the cows aren't really part of—" Albert began, but Trudy cut him off.

"I *said* she could go and gawk at the cows," Trudy repeated—pulling out her cell phone and flicking it open. "Is there going to be a problem, Albert?"

"No, Miss," he said hurriedly. "No problem at all."

Trudy snapped her phone shut and grinned at me.

"Off you go then," she said. "If I catch you near the stables again, I'll have Albert run you off with his pitchfork. Do you understand?"

I wasn't listening anymore. I was watching Albert shuffling away. He looked very suspicious. Once he was out of sight, I turned my attention back to Trudy. She was snorting through her nostrils at being made to wait.

"Whatever," I sighed and
casually strolled away.

I made my way toward the cow
field and then hid behind the wall
until Trudy finally trotted off on her
horse. I planned to double back and
carry out some stable surveillance. But
first, I needed a disguise.

Ducking into the empty cattle shed, I rummaged through my backpack.

Making room for the sketchbook and pencil decoy meant I didn't have many disguise options. I had to make do with a plastic nose, mustache and glasses (all in one), and an old cap. A glance in my mirror told me none of my flowery dresses would go with the mustache, but after a bit of snooping, I found an old brown coat hanging in the shed.

Pulling the coat on over my backpack to give myself a bit of a hunch, I stepped back into the yard and glanced around. I was about to head back for the stables when I heard a very strange sound coming from the field.

MOO-click-click!

MOO-click-click!

A small herd of cows were ambling awkwardly toward me, but there was something very odd about the way they moved, something creepy and clunky, like zombie cows.

The cows stopped suddenly
when they reached the fence and
peered at me through lifeless eyes. I'd
never seen a cow up close before, but
I was pretty sure they didn't tick—and
these cows were definitely ticking!

At first I thought they might be
time bombs made to look like cows,
but that didn't really make sense. So I
stood up on the fence, leaned over,
and tapped one firmly on the
head. It was rock hard and
echoed like a drum.
On closer
inspection, I
found that one of
the ears was not an
ear at all but a
large metal key!

Slipping through the fence, I gave the cow a quick once-over.

After a bit of expert tapping and knocking and banging, a small door clicked open in the cow's belly. Inside, I found a bunch of gears and wheels and pulleys whirring around. This definitely explained the ticking.

The cow was a
machine!

Slamming the door, I suddenly noticed that none of the clockwork cows actually had a tail. Instead, they each had a radio-controlled antenna with a tiny red light flashing at the end!

"Hmmm?" I thought to myself.

An antenna meant they were not just clockwork cattle that roamed the fields until their keys wound down.

That would be weird enough. No, these cows were actually being controlled by someone from a distance!

Slowly and discreetly I pulled out my mirror, held it up, and scanned the scene behind me. There in the stable courtyard was Albert the shifty stable hand! He was watching me closely while tapping away frantically inside his briefcase.

Suddenly all the cows clicked their heads in my direction.

"MOOOOO!" they boomed together and then started making their way forward again. Dropping the mirror, I leaped back over the fence just as the cows crashed through it!

Uh Oh!

In the courtyard, Albert had vanished around the back of the stables, so I ran after him as fast as my disguise would allow. Luckily, I was faster than the cows, who were very slow and ambled along like zombies.

Tucked away behind the stables, I found a chicken run. Albert was standing behind the hutch with his briefcase propped up against the roof.

I could now see that
it had an antenna
of its own
and was full
of dials and
buttons and
switches.

When he
saw me, he gave
an evil-genius smile and pressed one
of the buttons dramatically.

Cluck-click-click!

Cluck-click-click!

With a whirring of tiny gears
and wheels and pulleys, every chicken
in the yard stopped acting like
a chicken and snapped
its head in my
direction.

They flapped their
wings angrily and
began bobbing up
and down like
demented pogo sticks.

Glancing back around the stable,
I could see the herd of cows were still
bumbling across the yard. It wasn't
exactly a stampede, so I turned my
attention back to the chickens.

The bobbing seemed to be
powering up the springs in their legs
because one bird squatted down, a
click sounded, and then it launched
itself straight at me, snapping its beak
angrily.

Uh Oh!

Quick as a flash, I grabbed a nearby shovel. I smacked the ball of flapping metal before it could peck my plastic nose off.

I'm quite good at tennis so it shot across the yard like a rocket, landing with a massive

CLANG!

The pecking projectiles whizzed through the air one after another. I fended them off with my shovel. As the last of the clockwork chickens squatted, clicked, and launched, I turned sideways and whacked it in the direction of a very angry Albert.

The tin torpedo sailed through the air and crashed into the briefcase, knocking Albert off his feet.

The controls slid down the roof of the chicken coop. Albert lunged forward, but I was quicker and managed to snatch the briefcase.

"Give that back!" Albert growled, getting to his feet and dusting himself off.

I knew Albert was short, but he was a lot shorter than I'd realized.

In fact, he was so short that I could keep the briefcase from his reach just by holding it up in the air. Albert looked even more like an angry gnome jumping up and down trying to grab the briefcase.

Eventually the little man tired himself out.

"Now, why don't you start by telling me what you're up to?" I demanded.

Because I was taller, I felt like a grown-up dealing with a naughty child.

"Are you planning to take over the world?"

"Huh?" said Albert. He seemed genuinely surprised. "Of course not. . . ."

"Then what?" I said, stepping back and peering inside the briefcase.

"I'm planning to take over the *horse racing* world!" he stated proudly.

"On a metal chicken?" I said. I glanced back at the cows, who were now ambling around the corner and looking much more funny than scary. "Or on one of those?" I added with a smirk.

"Oh, those are just experiments," Albert said, shaking his head. "Now that I've perfected my mechanical-animal technology, there isn't a single horse that can beat Lightning."

"Lightning?" I gasped. "Trudy Hart's horse?"

"Lightning belongs to me!" snapped Albert. "That little brat thinks she owns everything just because her father owns the stables. But he's mine—I made every gear and spring."

"Lightning isn't even a real

horse?" I said. I was a little bit
impressed.

"No, in fact he's *better* than a real
horse!" said Albert
proudly.

Hearing the
familiar tick-tick-
ticking, I noticed that
the cows had
caught up with
me. I scanned the
control board
inside the
briefcase for the
Stop button.

It wasn't obvious what any of
the buttons did, but in the center was
a big red one. Criminal masterminds
and evil geniuses love big red buttons

in briefcases. The buttons usually mean something bad, like an explosion or an ejector seat or something like that. But seeing as though Albert wasn't technically trying to take over the world, I guessed that the big red button just meant "stop."

So I pressed it.

That was when lots of things happened all at once.

Albert leaped forward yelling,

"NOOOOOOOOO!"

The slow stampede of clockwork cows ground to a halt. Suddenly, each one exploded in a mass of springs and gears and little brass wheels.

Moments later, there was a very loud shriek. It came from the courtyard on the other side of the stables.

Even in all the chaos, I knew it belonged to Trudy Hart, because I've heard her shrieking loads of times before.

"What have you done?" Albert groaned, snatching the smoking briefcase and clutching it to his chest.

"Er, I'm not sure," I said awkwardly. "What *have* I done?"

"That was the *Self-Destruct* button," Albert sobbed, sinking helplessly to his knees. "It's linked to *all* the mechanical animals and was there only for an emergency! It was never supposed to be pressed!"

"Oh," I said feebly. "Sorry."

I did feel bad for breaking Albert's animals, but then I decided it was probably best to put an end to his plot. If he'd succeeded in taking over the racing world, he would most likely have turned his attention to the rest of the world.

It's best to nip these things in the bud.

Leaving Albert with his briefcase,

I decided to make my way back toward the petting zoo. Packing my disguise away, I draped the brown coat over the fence and stepped back through the stables.

In the middle of the courtyard sat a heap of machinery, springs, and metal horse parts. In the center of the mechanical mess sat Trudy. She was still perched in the saddle, holding onto the reins, angrily tapping the hide with her riding crop.

"Giddy up!" she demanded, as the metal torso creaked back and forth.

"Nice rocking horse," I said, slipping my sunglasses on with a smile.

The Case of the Perilous Pipe

"…So if you think about it, another day *really* won't make any difference," I pleaded. I was standing outside the school gates with my hands clasped hopefully. "I'm *already* a week behind."

"And that's exactly why you need to go back today," Mom said sternly.

"Your cold has gone and your temperature is back to normal. There's really no reason to keep you home from school a moment longer."

I coughed dramatically, but Mom just rolled her eyes.

"Have a nice day!" she said. She jumped back into the car and drove away.

I do like school, but I'd gotten used to sitting in bed watching TV and being waited on by Mom. It was also nice to have a break from being a secret agent and saving the world. I consoled myself with the fact that my first class of the day was music—something nice and relaxing to ease me back in.

Or so I thought!

In the week I'd been away, our old music teacher had retired and had been replaced by someone called Ms. Piper. In my experience, new teachers always spell trouble. They're usually quite clever and therefore prone to thoughts of world domination.

Admittedly, the tricky ones are mostly chemistry teachers or biology teachers. Even the odd math teacher can be found calculating mathematical formulas to take over the world.

I'd never actually heard of a music teacher being a criminal mastermind or an evil genius, but I decided to keep an eye on Ms. Piper just in case.

In class, I peered over my sunglasses as the new music teacher took off her coat and arranged books on her desk, which wasn't at all suspicious.

Then, after taking
attendance, she frowned.
She ran her finger back
down the list of names.

"Amelia Kidd?"
she said, narrowing
her eyes.

"Here!" I said,
just in case she
was taking
attendance
again.

"Yes, I know you're *here*,"
snapped Ms. Piper. "But it seems
you were not *here* for my
first lesson last week."

"I was sick," I
said. "But I'm pretty
sure I'll catch up."

"I'm *absolutely certain* you will catch up!" said Ms. Piper firmly. "Because when you return to this classroom at lunchtime, I will repeat the entire lesson to *ensure* you catch up!"

"Er…" I said, but she cut me off before I could come up with a decent excuse.

"Now, who can remind me of the wonderful tune we learned last week?" Ms. Piper demanded. She closed the attendance book and turned her attention to the rest of the class.

Everybody else's hand shot into the air and waved enthusiastically.

"Good," she said. She placed a long black case on her desk, flicked the clasp, and pulled out a funny-looking recorder. "Then you will have no trouble accompanying me on my medieval pipe."

Ms. Piper played three notes, and the class sang, "La! La! La!"

Not knowing the tune or the point of the lesson, all I could do was watch and listen, which was much more difficult than it sounds. The class sang the same three notes over and over again like a skipping CD. The sound of the weird wooden instrument made my brain itch.

With each chorus of "La! La! La!" my secret-agent instincts told me something strange was going on in the classroom. I just couldn't put my finger on exactly what it was.

"La! La! La!"

To begin with, everyone was very enthusiastic about the "La! La! La!" No one was fidgeting or getting bored. Also, everyone sang exactly in time with the pipe, which never happens with a bunch of kids singing together—unless they're in a choir, and even then. . . .

I turned my attention to Ms. Piper. She pursed her lips and shifted her fingers quickly on the pipe. Then I looked at the instrument itself. It was intricately carved and looked very old. It was probably an antique. . . .

An antique!

"Aha!" In my experience, antiques are *always* trouble. Whether they're cursed or enchanted or have spirits  trapped in them, you can't trust antiques.

But could the whole class *really* be under the influence of the pipe?

The "La! La! La!" ended abruptly, and every head turned in my direction.

"Amelia Kidd!" snapped the teacher. "Will you be joining in, or do you plan to continue gazing around the room like a clueless frog?"

Being a secret agent means you have to think fast, and my fast thoughts told me I could now find out for certain if the class was under the spell of the strange antique pipe.

I glanced over to Trudy Hart.

Having just been singled out by the teacher *and* called a clueless frog, I knew Trudy couldn't resist a sneer or a snigger.

Trudy looked back and gave me a friendly smile, but it wasn't a sarcastic friendly smile. It was a *genuine* friendly smile that made the hairs on

the back of my neck
stand on end.

The class was
definitely under the
spell of the pipe!

Ms. Piper
played the same
tune once again, and
the whole class sang it back
with perfect timing. She gave a
satisfied nod and then turned to me
with a raised eyebrow.

"La? La? La?" I
mumbled, uncertainly.

Ms. Piper
nodded again and was
about to resume playing
when the bell
sounded.

Immediately, the
whole class began
shifting and
fidgeting in their
chairs. It seemed
the bell had
broken the
trance. For
confirmation of this,
I turned to Trudy Hart.

   She immediately wrinkled her
nose and stuck her tongue out at me.

At recess I was sitting on a bench,
trying to work out how to get a
closer look at Ms. Piper's peculiar
pipe. Suddenly, the noise from the
playground was replaced by an eerie
silence.

I looked
around over my
sunglasses.

All the kids had mysteriously
stopped playing, running, and
screaming. They stood perfectly still like
statues. Then I heard a familiar tune
coming from the
window of the
music room.
I saw the
silhouette of
Ms. Piper and
her pipe.

"La! La! La!"   "La! La! La!"

Singing the song of the distant pipe, the whole playground turned to face me. Everyone began walking in my direction, and not just the kids from *my* music class. It was every kid in the school.

Everyone except me was under Ms. Piper's spell!

Realizing the music teacher was on to me, I grabbed my backpack and was about to run, when another sound echoed through the playground—the bell signaling the end of recess.

All the kids stopped, looked around, and began scratching their heads.

The bell had broken the spell again, but it was too close for comfort. Pulling on my backpack, I hurried back into school. I ran straight to the next class on my schedule.

It was computer studies, and I had some research to do!

After a week away from school, I knew I'd be a bit behind on most of my subjects, but computer studies wasn't one of them. Secret agents have to be super quick on computers, so I'm always ahead of everyone else. I planned to use that time to find out about medieval pipes and the mysterious Ms. Piper.

It took me a while, but after a lot of digging, I found a picture of Ms. Piper's pipe. It was called the Perilous Pipe, and loads of historical documents mentioned it. As I suspected, the instrument was enchanted. That meant a spell had been cast on it back in the days when people cast spells.

The Perilous Pipe had been enchanted nearly three hundred years ago—or rather the reed that makes the sound *inside* the pipe had been enchanted. What was interesting was that it had originally belonged to someone called The Piper!

Which was all a bit too much of a coincidence if you ask me.

I made another search.

There were lots of different references to The Piper. Some were stories, and others were real historical accounts from old newspapers and journals. The one thing they all had in common was what The Piper was famous for.

He was famous for leading children away using the Perilous Pipe!

I even found an old-fashioned drawing of The Piper, and the resemblance made me gasp out loud.

I glanced up from
the screen to make sure
no one had heard me.
I was just in time
to see Ms. Piper
creeping past the
window with a large pair
of bolt cutters!

This made me
gasp even louder!

"Amelia?" said Mr.
Moore. "Are you feeling well?"

The tech
teacher looked
concerned and
started weaving
through the
computer desks
toward me.

Thinking fast, I quickly cleared the screen and pulled a big wad of tissues out of my backpack.
I wiped my nose and peered helplessly up at him.

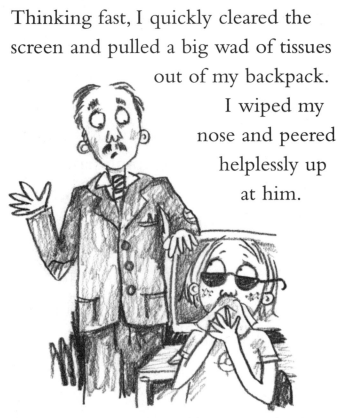

"Just a few sniffles!" I sighed, glancing sideways at the clock.

It was ten minutes to lunchtime, and I decided I could use those ten minutes to snoop around Ms. Piper's classroom. Taking a deep breath, I launched an enormous coughing fit into my tissues.

"Oh, dear!" said Mr. Moore. "I think you should take yourself to see the nurse immediately."

Pulling on my backpack, I nodded bravely and headed for the door, throwing in a couple of sniffs for good measure. Once out of sight, I pocketed the tissues and bolted.

Backing along the wall of the corridor, I peered through the door of the music room. There were no lessons going on inside, but Ms. Piper had already returned. She was standing at the window looking out into the playground where I'd seen her at break time.

On her desk lay the Perilous Pipe.

This was my chance!

Opening the door quietly, I crept into the classroom. I tiptoed toward the desk, but I'd only made it halfway before Ms. Piper spoke. She startled me, and I froze to the spot.

"The mark of a truly gifted musician is excellent hearing," said Ms. Piper. She turned around dramatically and glanced at her watch. "You're early!"

I smiled innocently and shrugged.

Ms. Piper narrowed her eyes.

"*Why* are you early?" she added suspiciously.

Our eyes met over the Perilous Pipe. The expression on Ms. Piper's face changed, and I realized she was on to me. We both ran for the pipe at the same time. Ms. Piper was much taller, so I knew she'd get there first.

I reached into my pocket, hoping I'd left a small gadget there or *something* I could use to even the odds. All I found was the wad of tissues.

Not ideal, but I threw them at her
anyway.

"URRRRGGGH!" she
shrieked. She batted the air angrily as
the tissue storm surrounded her. The
tissues were actually clean, but Ms.

Piper didn't know that. I quickly scrabbled onto the desk and searched for the pipe. But as the last of the tissues fluttered down, I saw that it was gone.

"Looking for this?" smiled Ms. Piper. She was waving the weird wooden instrument in the air triumphantly.

"You won't get away with it!" I said angrily.

"Oh, don't bother trying to get me to rant about my plans," she said dismissively. "I'm going to steal all the children away with my pipe and then hold them for ransom. It's that simple really."

I'd never met any evil geniuses or a criminal masterminds who didn't like ranting about their evil plans, so this took me by surprise.

The taking-over-the-world rant usually gives me time to come up with a strategy, but Ms. Piper didn't waste time.

She lifted the pipe to her lips and began playing.

I still hadn't been brainwashed by the tune, but the sound filtered out of the classroom. I heard chairs scraping across the floor all over the school, followed by the sound of footsteps marching toward the music room.

Soon the corridor outside filled
with kids. Trudy Hart was right at the
front wearing that creepy, friendly
smile.

My only chance for escape was
the lunchtime bell breaking the spell. I
looked at the clock and saw more
than ten minutes had passed since
leaving the computer room.

The bell should have sounded
already!

"Ring! Ring! It's lunchtime!" sang Ms. Piper. "And now I think it's time for you to catch up with the rest of your class," she added, shifting her fingers along the pipe and pursing her lips.

Now I knew what Ms. Piper had been doing with the bolt cutters! Seeing the flaw in her plan at recess, she'd crept around the school and disconnected all the bells.

I looked around frantically for an escape route, but the kids were blocking the door and the windows were too high up. I tried to remember our last fire drill. I thought there was an emergency exit somewhere nearby. . . .

Fire drill! I tipped my sunglasses and smiled at Ms. Piper.

My smile obviously took her by surprise because she paused for a moment. In that moment, I snatched the Perilous Pipe and whacked it against the fire alarm. Then I sprinted for the door.

As the sound of the fire alarm bell filled the hallway, the kids began scratching their heads. As I barged past Trudy, I was relieved to see her sticking her tongue out at me.

Confused teachers were flapping their arms amid the sea of equally confused kids. They were trying to organize the fire drill. In all the chaos, no one noticed as I ducked down and rummaged in my backpack.

Tucking my hair up inside a baseball cap, I quickly blended back into the crowd. We were led outside to form orderly lines.

I kept my head down and the pipe behind my back as Ms. Piper stalked the lines of kids. She walked straight past me twice, thinking I was just one of many boys in baseball caps.

When the fire alarm stopped, the teachers spread out and took attendance. Peering under the brim of my cap, I saw Ms. Piper abandon her search and smile to herself as the names were called.

As *K* for Kidd drew nearer, I racked my brain, thinking about the research and the stories and the enchantment.... Aha! I thought, blindly fiddling with the pipe behind my back.

"Amelia Kidd?" called Mr. Moore.

"Here!" I said, slipping off the baseball cap.

Ms. Piper leaped forward, shoved Mr. Moore out of the way, and snatched the pipe from behind my back.

"You fool!" she yelled, jabbing the antique instrument in my direction like a sword. "You thought you could prevent *me* from taking over the world?"

"Excuse me?" said Mr. Moore, frowning at Ms. Piper.

"Yes, you heard me correctly," snapped the music teacher. "I plan to take over the world. It is a genius plan involving my enchanted pipe...."

It seemed Ms. Piper couldn't resist a rant after all. She ranted on and on and on, revealing every part of her plot for world domination.

It was actually one of the longest rants I've ever heard from an evil genius or criminal mastermind.

Of course everyone was looking at Ms. Piper as though she'd gone mad, especially when she lifted the pipe to her lips, positioned her hands over the appropriate holes, and blew…and no sound came out.

There was a scuffle when Ms. Piper lunged for me, but she was quickly restrained. She was taken away yelling about interfering little hooligans and magical pipes and stolen enchanted reeds.

A few kids giggled. The teachers shook their heads sadly.

When Mom picked me up, she asked if I'd missed anything interesting during my week off sick. Pulling the enchanted reed from my back pocket, I tipped my glasses and studied it closely. It was obviously harmless without the pipe. I snapped the reed in half and flicked the pieces out of the window.

"Not really," I said, smiling to myself. "But it's *definitely* good to be back."

The Case of the Creepy Cakes

On Saturdays, Mom takes me to the bakery around the corner and we treat ourselves to a jelly donut or a fresh cupcake. We've done it for as long as I can remember. I always look forward to it.

Or at least I *used* to look forward to it....

In the week since our last visit, the bakery had mysteriously closed

down and reopened. It was now called
The Beauty Sisters' Cake Emporium.
It was a bit of a flashy name for a
bakery if you ask me.

But the shop wasn't the only
thing that was different.

"Look at the size of those
donuts!" Mom squealed as we passed
the window of the shop.

THE BEAUTY SISTERS' CAKE EMPORIUM

"They must be twice the size of the old ones. They're half the price too!" she gasped.

I tipped my glasses and peered at the selection of cakes.

It was true, the donuts were massive—in fact, all the cakes in the window were freakishly huge. There were enormous eclairs, colossal cupcakes, mammoth meringues—and all at half the regular price.

My first instinct was to get excited like Mom had, but then my secret-agent instincts kicked in. I viewed the cakes with suspicion. I wanted to know *why* the cakes were so big, *why* they were so cheap, and *who* were the strangely generous Beauty Sisters?

Because evil
geniuses and criminal
masterminds don't
usually hang out in
bakeries, I hadn't
brought my backpack
full of gadgets. But I

still had my sunglasses. I adjusted them
carefully to conceal my identity and
slipped into the shop.

Any hope of going unnoticed while carrying out preliminary surveillance was foiled when Mom entered the shop behind me. She clapped her hands together loudly.

"I THINK I'VE JUST DIED AND GONE TO HEAVEN!" she shrieked. She gazed with wide eyes at shelves stuffed with every kind of sweet known to man.

Behind the counter, the heads of two thin figures snapped in our direction. For a fraction of a second, the elderly pair narrowed their eyes. Then they quickly stretched their mouths into wide, friendly smiles.

"Welcome to The Beauty Sisters' Cake Emporium!" they sang, ignoring me to focus their greeting on Mom.

I took my chance to size them up without drawing attention to myself.

The first remarkable thing about the Beauty Sisters was that they were identical twins. Everything about them was a mirror image and probably had been for about a hundred years. They both looked ancient.

The second remarkable thing was how they were dressed.

As they stepped out from behind the counter, the pair were both unbelievably glamorous. But it wasn't the usual funky-grandma kind of glamour. This was full-on catwalk glamour, complete with crazy clothes, huge hairdos, and tons of bright makeup.

Mom's wide eyes grew a little wider when confronted with the Beauty Sisters. For a moment she seemed unable to speak at all.

"Goodness me," she gasped eventually. "You're both, er..."

"Beautiful?" the sisters chimed together. "Yes, we know."

"Um, yes!" Mom stammered. "That's *exactly* what I was about to say!"

"We used to be supermodels, you know," the pair stated proudly.

While the grown-ups made small talk, I scanned the shop for signs of criminal activity. But aside from the size of the cakes, there was nothing out of the ordinary, except for the peculiar-looking twins.

"And however do you both stay so slim?" Mom laughed. "If I had a shop like this, I'd be tempted to eat cake all day long," she added and then laughed some more.

The twins were not laughing at Mom's joke. In fact, they'd stopped smiling altogether. Their identical faces suddenly wore the same grave expression.

"We *never* eat the cakes," they hissed. The sisters hurried back behind

the counter and busied themselves by
working on a display of giant apple
fritters.

"Oh," said Mom, to fill the
awkward silence.

While Mom tried to work out
what she'd said wrong, I crept over
to the counter. Tipping my sunglasses,

I watched as the angry twins
whispered to each other while
frantically tying pink bows around
bags of sweets.

Suddenly two pairs of eyes glared in my direction.

"What do you want, little girl?" they said in unison.

"Two donuts, please!" I said and did my best innocent smile.

Back home,
I eyed the bag of
donuts on the
kitchen counter.
They did look and
smell delicious, but
I didn't plan on
Mom or me
eating them. The

Beauty Sisters were up to something.
They were probably trying to take
over the world. I was certain the
baked goods were part of the plan.

I studied the contents of the
paper bag and wondered what an evil
genius or a criminal mastermind
could possibly do with a donut.
The answer seemed pretty obvious
to me.

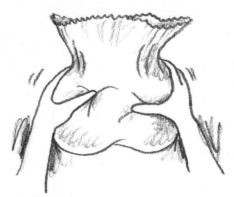

Holding the bag at arm's length, I gripped each donut through the paper. I began a slow, careful squeeze. Then, with my face still tense because I half-expected the donuts to explode, I peered into the bag. I was a bit disappointed to see two saggy donuts and a bag full of jelly filling.

Hmmm?

I dipped my finger in the sticky red goo and held it up to my nose. It smelled OK, but I still didn't want to eat it. Instead, I pulled out my magnifying glass and moved to the window for a closer look.

It was then that something strange happened: as the heat from the sun intensified through the magnifying glass, the jam started bubbling and expanding right before my eyes!

"Heat!" I gasped.

I flicked the red blob away, grabbed the donut bag, and plopped it on the hot radiator. The jam in the bag immediately began to swell. It strained at the paper bag. Then it rose up like a fizzy can of soda. Thinking fast, I ran to the trash. I threw the whole thing in just as the paper burst. The red mess spilled everywhere.

"What on earth?" yelled Mom, appearing in the doorway.

"Er, I dropped our donuts in the trash . . . *accidentally*," I stammered, although given more time, I would definitely have come up with a better excuse.

Mom gazed at the red mess in the trash.

"And they look like really gooey ones too," she sighed.

"I'll run back to the shop!" I said quickly. "My treat!" And before Mom could answer, I grabbed my backpack and bolted for the door. Around the corner, I stopped to check my supplies. Without time to prepare, I wasn't sure what disguises I'd packed. All I could find was a beret and a flowery scarf that I'd collected because I might need to look like a French lady one day.

It was not ideal, but it would have to do.

Walking slowly past the window of the cake shop, I spied the Beauty Sisters. They were busy talking to customers at the counter. I took the chance to slip into the shop. Once inside, I edged my way quietly along the wall. I pretended to browse the shelves, while secretly heading for a curtain at the back.

With one last glance to make sure the twins were still distracted, I was about to duck through the curtain when a terrifying noise stopped me in my tracks.

"BUT I WANT IT NOOOOOW!" screamed a strangely familiar voice.

I froze to the spot.

Pulling my beret down and my scarf up, I turned my head again slowly. The other customers in the shop were actually my archenemy, Trudy Hart, and her tired-looking parents.

Trudy is in my class at school, but we don't get along. She's very spoiled and used to getting her way. Today, that meant screaming and stamping her foot in the middle of the shop while her parents tried to calm her down.

Typical! I thought.

Then I realized that because Trudy was having a tantrum, everyone's attention was on her. No one was looking at me. So I shrugged my shoulders and stepped casually through the curtain.

I'd never seen the back of a bakery before. I didn't really know what to expect, but I definitely didn't expect to find what I found. The back of The Beauty Sisters' Cake Emporium looked exactly like a mad scientist's laboratory!

There were test tubes and lightning rods and smoking beakers. Among all the complicated scientific

equipment were bags of sugar, sacks of flour, cans of cream, and jars of jam. There was also a light frost covering everything because the room was as cold as a freezer.

Hmmm? I thought, rubbing my arms for warmth.

My plan to get into the back of the shop didn't really cover what I would do once I got there. I decided to snoop around a bit. I hoped to discover exactly what the Beauty Sisters were plotting.

Then I'd find a way to stop them.

I could hear Trudy still
screaming her demands in the shop. I
knew she would continue to scream
until she got her own way. I began a
thorough search of the weird cake
laboratory.

I started with the diagrams on
the wall.

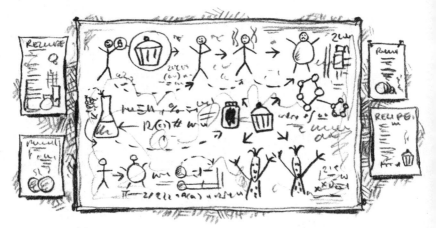

As far as I could tell from the
drawings, the twins were filling their
cakes with specially modified fillings

that would instantly make people gain weight. Very odd. I'd foiled some strange attempts to take over the world before, but this was definitely one of the strangest.

I also worked out from the diagrams that body heat made the fillings swell. This explained why my tampering with the donuts had set off the weird expanding jelly. Since bodies aren't as hot as radiators, people probably wouldn't explode.

They would just get very,
very big!

Scattered around the room were
large crates filled with cakes and other
treats, but it was so cold in the lab, I
decided they were probably harmless
so long as I didn't eat them or warm
them up. Then I noticed a table in the
middle of the room with a large cloth
draped over it.

There was no way of knowing what was underneath. It could have been a booby trap, so I pulled out my extendable grabber-hand gadget (it's basically a hand on a stick). I carefully removed the cloth.

Underneath the cloth was the biggest layer cake I'd ever seen! It was about half my size and stuffed to bursting with filling and frosting. Then I peered down at the cake and gasped out loud.

The words "Happy Birthday
Trudy" glared back at me in bright
pink frosting!

I could have kicked myself for
not making the connection earlier.

Trudy had made a big fuss all
week at school about her birthday
party. She even held a meeting in the
playground where the exclusive party
invitations were handed out. She also
provided a typed list of acceptable
birthday presents.

Needless to say, I didn't get an invitation. Now I was staring at her birthday cake.

Suddenly everything went eerily silent. I realized the sound of Trudy screaming and stamping had stopped. This could mean only one thing. Either Trudy had just got her way, or she'd left the shop quietly *without* getting her way.

I knew Trudy well enough to know which was most likely and turned around to find two thin figures looming in the doorway!

"Er... *bonjour!*" I said quickly, in my best French accent. "*Croissants?*" I added hopefully, having just used up all the French words I knew.

The twins eyed me up and
down and then scuttled forward.

"You're not French," said the twin on the left.

"You're not chic enough," added the twin on the right.

I backed away slowly and tried to think fast.

One sure way to buy time with criminal masterminds is to get them ranting about their plans for world domination. Most of them can't resist telling you how clever they think they are.

"You won't get away with it!" I said, which is usually a good trigger.

The twins stopped and frowned at each other. The pair had seen right through my disguise so perhaps they were too smart to fall for the rant trigger. Having backed myself into the corner of the room, I could only wait and hold my breath.

"We WILL get away with it!"
they yelled in unison. "Once the
world gets a taste of our delicious
cakes, they'll all puff up like
marshmallows, and soon EVERYONE
will be a big roly-poly dumpling...."

While the Beauty Sisters
continued to rant, I looked around
frantically. The twins were blocking
the door, so there was no way out.

I had to cause a diversion to get past them.

My eyes fell on the thermostat mounted on the wall beside me.

"Aha!" I said to myself, because if I said it out loud it would completely give the plan away. Aiming carefully, I flicked the lever on my extendable grabber-hand and

spun the dial from "Arctic" to "Tropical." I tucked the gadget away again in the blink of an eye.

"And when everyone else is waddling around like great big balloons, WE will be the only THIN ones. Then the fashion world will have no choice but to make us supermodels again!" concluded the Beauty Sisters.

"Not bad," I said. I said it out loud because I needed to buy more time. "Except for one tiny flaw," I added, casually loosening

my scarf because the room was already heating up.

"What flaw?" asked the twins suspiciously. "Our plan is flawless, like us!"

"You didn't count on *me* stopping you!" I said firmly.

Suddenly a cream-filled donut exploded in the corner

of the room, splurting its
filling right across the
ceiling. It was followed by
another and another. Then whole
trays of donuts and cupcakes started
blowing up all over the place.

BANG!

BANG!

BANG!

SPLAT! SPLAT! SPLAT!

The twins gripped each other and shrieked with each explosion. I wrapped myself in the cloth and headed for the door, ducking and diving through the crossfire of flying fillings.

I was halfway to freedom when the explosions suddenly stopped. All that remained was the foaming fillings, flowing from the trays.

The angry twins lunged forward, but I ducked behind the table in the middle of the room.

Now the only thing that stood between the twins and me was the giant layer cake. Glancing down, I saw that it was already beginning to throb. The Beauty Sisters had seen it too because they were backing away.

Thinking on my feet, I grabbed the giant cake, heaved it above my head and took off after them. This was difficult because the cake was really heavy.

Then as soon as I was close enough, I threw the cake as hard as I could.

I watched in slow motion as the cake sailed through the air, but the twins were quick and managed to duck down just in time. The giant cake flew over their heads, through the curtain, and out into the shop.

BANG! SPLAT!

The explosion made the curtain
flap inward, and through the gap, I
saw a Trudy-shaped tower of frosting
with sponge cake on top.

This was quickly followed by an ear-piercing squeal that made the windows rattle.

Trudy did look funny covered in cake, but there was no time to enjoy it. The twins had picked themselves up. They now looked even meaner than before. I glanced around frantically and grabbed the nearest things to hand.

Two squeezy bags of bright pink frosting!

With an expert flick of my wrists, I cocked the frosting bags and aimed them steadily at the twins. The Beauty Sisters immediately put their hands up in surrender. This was good because that's when Trudy's parents appeared through the curtain. They were eager to know why their daughter was buried under a giant cake.

When you're a secret agent, you can't hang around and take credit for saving the world. Because all the evidence was there in the cake lab, I quickly armed Mr. and Mrs. Hart with the frosting bags and made my getaway.

I couldn't risk revealing my identity as I passed the creamy, jammy mountain in the middle of the shop. But as two furious eyes peered out at me, I couldn't resist a quick comment either.

"*Bonjour, croissant!*" I said, in my best French accent, and then I jogged home.

AGENTAmelia

Check out my other books!

#1 Ghost Diamond
#2 Zombie Cows
#3 Hypno Hounds
#4 Spooky Ballet

Three more
fabulously funny
stories in each book.